This book belongs to:

....

....

The

Geronimo Stilton

Cookbook

Fun recipes for parents and kids to cook together, with terrific tips from Geronimo!

Scholastic Inc.

New York   Toronto   London   Auckland   Sydney
Mexico City   New Delhi   Hong Kong   Buenos Aires

Library of Congress Cataloging-in-Publication Data

Stilton, Geronimo.
   [Cucina Italiana. English]
   Geronimo Stilton's cookbook: fun recipes for kids and parents to cook together, with terrific tips from Geronimo Stilton.
      p. cm.
   ISBN 0-439-82549-0
   1. Cookery.   I. Title.
   TX652.S75 2005
   641.5--dc22
         2005020344

Copyright © 2005 - La Cucina Italiana/Editrice Quadratum - Edizioni Piemme S.p.A., Via del Carmine 5, 15033 Casale Monferrato (AL), Italia.

English translation © 2005 - La Cucina Italiana/Editrice Quadratum - Edizioni Piemme S.p.A.

GERONIMO STILTON names, characters, and related indicia are copyright, trademark, and exclusive license of Edizioni Piemme S.p.A. All rights reserved. The moral right of the author has been asserted.

Published by Scholastic Inc.
SCHOLASTIC and associated logos are trademarks and/or registered trademarks of Scholastic Inc.

Stilton is the name of a famous English cheese. It is a registered trademark of the Stilton Cheese Makers' Association. For more information, go to www.stiltoncheese.com.

Original title: *Faccia di crema, ricette divertenti per i bambini*
Photos and Recipes © La Cucina Italiana/Editrice Quadratum
Geronimo Stilton illustrations & graphics © Edizioni Piemme
Graphics by: Laura Zuccotti
Special thanks to Lidia Morson Tramontozzi, Kathryn Cristaldi, and Margaret Happel Perry

12 11 10 9 8 7 6 5 4 3 2 1   5 6 7 8 9 10/0

Printed in Mexico
First printing, December 2005

Contents

Introduction

Imagine What You Can Do!

Holey cheese — there are so many wonderful things that you can create in the kitchen! And by cooking yummy food, you can also express your creativity. If you look at all of the things in your kitchen (pots, pans, blenders, oven, knives, spoons), they make up a kind of laboratory where you can wash, slice, cook, and transform different foods into vegetable boats, colorful clown pizzas, and happy-face cookies! And there are many ways to substitute in healthier ingredients, too. For example, try low-fat cheese on your pizza! It's fun to experiment with new things.

But you always need to put safety first. Inexperienced cooks can get themselves in a lot of trouble in the kitchen! So above all else, you need to know your laboratory very well. Here are a few important rules to follow.

Tools Are Not Toys

Be sure to enter the kitchen slowly, and always move carefully. To make cooking really fun, you have to take it seriously. Kitchen tools are not toys — some are even dangerous! Make sure there is always an adult around to help you. And whenever you see this icon you *must* ask for an adult's help. Together, decide which tools you can use alone, and which ones the adult should use. Me? I don't like using sharp knives. I'm too fond of my tail!

Cooking Rules by the Dozen

To work well in the kitchen, you should remember some basic rules.

1. Always ask an adult for help before you begin each recipe. Read each recipe together before starting.

2. Wash your hands thoroughly with soap, and put on an apron so your clothes don't get dirty. You should always be squeaky-clean when you're cooking!

3. Check to make sure you have all of the ingredients and tools you need before you begin to cook.

4. Measure and prepare all ingredients using the appropriate tools.

5. Don't cut any food directly on the table or countertop. Use a cutting board instead.

6. Always work slowly and calmly. Never use knives unless an adult says it's OK, and always hold them carefully by the handle. If you're not comfortable handling something, an adult should help you.

7. When putting anything in or taking anything out of the oven, always use oven mitts, and make sure an adult is nearby.

8. Be very careful near the stove, or near pots or pans that are hot. Make sure that the pot or pan's handle is not sticking out where you might bump into it, but is turned toward the inside of the stove.

9. When stirring or mixing, always hold the pot, pan, or bowl with one hand to keep it from slipping.

10. Never leave a pot on the stove unattended, and always check to make sure your food isn't overcooking. When you are finished cooking, be sure to turn off the stove, oven, or grill.

11. If something spills on the floor while you're working, clean it up immediately. That way, you won't fall and hurt yourself!

12. Refrigerate any leftovers. They'll be delicious later! *Are you ready? Let's cook!*

Cheesy, Cheerful Pizzas

Pizza is delicious, but it's also fun to make, especially when you put together pizzas with the funniest faces imaginable! You can make your pizzas look like clowns, cats, clocks, owls, and lots of other things. You'll find some suggestions here, but you can always use your imagination to come up with lots of other ideas that are silly *and* tasty!

Before you begin you may want to make your own pizza dough — see page 68. Or if you are in a hurry, go to the store and buy a 1-pound package of ready-made pizza dough. The dough will make four individual pizzas. They can all be the same or they can all be different. Just follow the recipes and pictures to make the pizzas that you like best. But be sure to ask your family and friends to help you eat them!

Trap's "Clowning Around" Pizza

1. Divide the dough into 4 even pieces. On a lightly floured surface, knead and roll each piece into a ball. Cover the balls with a clean, damp dishtowel. Set in a warm place for 20 minutes for the dough to rise. Heat the oven to 450° F.

2. To make each clown pizza: On a lightly floured surface, roll and stretch 1 ball of dough into a 6- to 8-inch circle. Place on an oiled baking sheet. Spread ¼ cup tomato sauce, or more, over the dough, leaving a ½-inch rim around the edge. Drizzle the pizza with a little olive oil, and sprinkle with ¼ teaspoon of oregano. Bake the pizza for 10 minutes until the crust is crisp and golden. Carefully remove the pizza from the oven. Let pizza cool for 5 minutes until it is safe to handle. Lower the oven temperature to 350° F. Place the remaining ingredients on the pizza (see photo).

3. Use 3 slices of mozzarella to make the mouth and ears: Use a whole slice for the mouth and half slices for the ears. Cut circles from the third slice and use for the cheeks.

4. Use red bell peppers to make the lips, bow tie, and to decorate the ears: Cut out lip shape; place on the mozzarella mouth. Cut out bow-tie shape; place under the mouth. Place 2 small strips on the ears.

5. Use zucchini to make the eyes and hair: Use 2 small round zucchini circles for eyes. Top with tiny circles cut from zucchini skin. Cut 2-inch-long strips from remaining zucchini; set between the ears to make hair.

6. Use tomatoes to decorate the cheeks: Cut in half and set on top of cheeks.

7. Use pitted green olives to make the nose and to decorate the eyes and bow tie: Cut olives in half crosswise; use one half as the nose. Cut 3 thin olive circles; set 2 in center of zucchini eyes. Place third olive circle in center of bow tie.

8. Bake the pizza for 5 minutes more, or until the cheese just starts to melt.

9. Repeat to make 3 more pizzas. Turn off the oven, and serve the pizzas while warm.

Ingredients

Makes 4 individual pizzas

Prep and cook time: 1 hour

- Pizza Dough, see recipe page 68, or one 1-pound package refrigerated ready-made pizza dough
- Flour, for work surface
- Oil, for baking sheet
- 1 cup prepared tomato sauce, or more to taste
- Extra-virgin olive oil
- 1 teaspoon crushed oregano leaves, or to taste
- One 8-ounce package of mozzarella
- 2 small red bell peppers
- 2 small zucchini
- 4 cherry tomatoes
- 4 pitted green olives

Yummy!

Geronimo Stilton's Advice

Cooking can be lots of fun, but don't be a cheesebrain. Always make sure there's an adult at home to give you a **paw**. Before starting, gather all of the ingredients and cooking tools. After you're done using each tool, wash it and put it away. When you are finished cooking, your kitchen will be **SQUEAKY CLEAN!**

The Mouse Ran Up the Clock Pizza

1. Divide the dough into 4 even pieces. On a lightly floured surface, knead and roll each piece into a ball. Cover the balls with a clean, damp dish-towel. Set in a warm place for 20 minutes for the dough to rise. Heat the oven to 450° F.

2. To make each clock pizza: On a lightly floured surface, roll and stretch 1 ball of dough into a 6- to 8-inch circle. Place on an oiled baking sheet. Spread ¼ cup tomato sauce, or more, over the dough, leaving a ½-inch rim around the edge. Drizzle the pizza with a little olive oil, and sprinkle with ¼ teaspoon of oregano. Bake the pizza for 10 minutes until the crust is crisp and golden. Carefully remove the pizza from the oven and let cool for 5 minutes until safe to handle. Lower the oven temperature to 350° F. Place remaining ingredients on the pizza (see photo).

3. Use 2 slices of mozzarella to decorate the clock: Using 1- or 1-½-inch round cookie cutter, cut 4 circles from the cheese slices. Place them on the pizza at 12-, 3-, 6-, and 9-o'clock positions.

4. Use 4 slices of fontina or Muenster cheese to decorate the clock: Using 1- or 1-½-inch cookie cutter, cut 8 circles from the cheese slices. Place 2 circles between each mozzarella circle.

5. Use 2 hot dogs to decorate the clock and make the hands: Cut 1 hot dog into 12 circles. Top each cheese circle with a hot dog circle. Cut the second hot dog in half lengthwise. With a sharp, pointy knife, cut each half into the hand of a clock and set on the pizza.

6. Use 2 pitted black olives, cut lengthwise, to decorate the clock: Set 3 halves on top of mozzarella circles.

7. Use 2 thin red bell pepper strips to decorate the clock: Cut 1 strip into tiny dots; set in place. Cut the second strip into 4 pieces. Arrange the pieces to make the Roman numeral XII on the top of the clock. Bake the pizza for 5 minutes more or until the cheese just starts to melt.

8. Repeat to make 3 more pizzas. Turn off the oven, and serve the pizzas while warm.

Ingredients

Makes 4 individual pizzas

Prep and cook time: 1 hour

- Pizza Dough, see recipe page 68, or one 1-pound package of refrigerated ready-made pizza dough
- Flour, for work surface
- Oil, for baking sheet
- 1 cup prepared tomato sauce, or more to taste
- Extra-virgin olive oil
- 1 teaspoon crushed oregano leaves, or to taste
- One 8-ounce package of mozzarella
- One 8-ounce package of fontina or Muenster cheese
- 8 cooked hot dogs
- 6 small pitted black olives
- 1 small red bell pepper

Time to eat!

Geronimo Stilton's Advice

Whipping up a favorite meal for a friend or family member can make you feel all *warm and furry* inside. When Benjamin was learning how to tell time, I made him a clock pizza. He loved *every minute* of it! Yum!

Geronimo's 'Fraidy Cat Pizza

1. Divide the dough into 4 even pieces. On a lightly floured surface, knead and roll each piece into a ball. Cover the balls with a clean, damp dishtowel. Set in a warm place for 20 minutes for the dough to rise. Heat the oven to 450° F.

2. To make each cat pizza: On a floured surface, roll and stretch 1 ball of dough into a 6- to 8-inch circle. Place on an oiled baking sheet. Spread ¼ cup tomato sauce, or more, over the dough, leaving a ½-inch rim around the edge. Drizzle the pizza with a little olive oil, and sprinkle with ¼ teaspoon of oregano. Bake the pizza for 10 minutes until the crust is crisp and golden. Carefully remove the pizza from the oven. Let it cool 5 minutes until it is safe to handle. Lower the oven temperature to 350° F. Place the remaining ingredients on the pizza (see photo).

3. Use 3 slices of mozzarella to make the cat's ears and mouth: Use 2 slices to make the cat's ears. Cut the third slice into a smaller circle to make the cat's mouth.

4. Use 1 hot dog to make the cat's whiskers: Cut a round slice from the end of the hot dog; set aside. Cut six 3-inch strips from the hot dog. Place strips on the pizza to form whiskers. Top with a hot dog slice.

5. Use 1 each of the pitted black and green olives, and a red pepper slice to decorate the cat face: Cut the black olive in half; set in place for the eyes. Cut the green olive in half; set one half in place for the mouth. Place the red pepper slice under the green olive half to form the lip.

6. Use 2 mushroom slices for the top of the ears. Bake the pizza for 5 minutes more or until the cheese just starts to melt.

7. Repeat to make 3 more pizzas. Turn off the oven, and serve the pizzas while warm.

Enjoy!

Ingredients

Makes 4 individual pizzas

Prep and cook time: 1 hour

- Pizza Dough, see recipe page 68, *or* one 1-pound package of refrigerated ready-made pizza dough
- Flour, for work surface
- Oil, for baking sheet
- 1 cup prepared tomato sauce, *or* more to taste
- Extra-virgin olive oil
- 1 teaspoon crushed oregano leaves, *or* to taste
- One 8-ounce package of mozzarella
- 4 cooked hot dogs
- 4 pitted black olives
- 2 pitted green olives
- 1 small red bell pepper
- 1 small mushroom, cut in slices

Geronimo Stilton's Advice

Cooking with dirty **paws** is like blowing your snout without using a tissue! That's why the very FIRST thing you must do before starting to cook is to wash up. It's also a good idea to put on an apron. That way you won't get your clothes all messy. My uncle Hotpaws wears a **silly apron** at our family barbecues. It has a picture of a smiling mouse juggling kittens on it!

Thea's Rowdy Rabbit Pizza

1. Divide the dough into 4 even pieces. On a lightly floured surface, knead and roll each piece into a ball. Cover the balls with a clean, damp dishtowel. Set in a warm place for 20 minutes for the dough to rise. Heat the oven to 450° F.

2. To make each rabbit pizza: On a lightly floured surface, roll and stretch 1 ball of dough into a 6- to 8-inch circle. Place on an oiled baking sheet. Spread ¼ cup tomato sauce, or more, over the dough, leaving a ½-inch rim around the edge. Drizzle the pizza with a little olive oil, and sprinkle with ¼ teaspoon of oregano. Bake the pizza for 10 minutes until the crust is crisp and golden. Carefully remove the pizza from the oven. Let pizza cool for 5 minutes until it is safe to handle. Lower the oven temperature to 350° F. Place the remaining ingredients on the pizza (see photo).

3. Use 3 slices of mozzarella to make the head and cheeks: Set the slices in the center of the pizza to form a forehead and two cheeks.

4. Use ¼ cup cooked broccoli florets to make the hair: Place along the top edge of the cheese slice.

5. Use 3 cooked round carrot slices to make the eyes and rabbit tongue: Tuck 2 slices on top of the cheeks for the eyes. Set the third slice in the center where the cheeks join to make the tongue.

6. Use 1 pitted black olive and a cherry tomato to make the eyes and nose: Cut 1 olive in half; place in the center of each eye at the bottom. Set the whole cherry tomato below the eyes to make the nose. Bake the pizza for 5 minutes more, or until the cheese just starts to melt. Just before serving, tuck a few chive strands under each side of the nose to form the whiskers.

7. Repeat to make 3 more pizzas. Turn off the oven, and serve the pizzas while warm.

Ingredients

Makes 4 individual pizzas

Prep and cook time: 1 hour

- Pizza Dough, see recipe page 68, *or* one 1-pound package of refrigerated ready-made pizza dough
- Flour, for work surface
- Oil, for baking sheet
- 1 cup prepared tomato sauce, *or* more to taste
- Extra-virgin olive oil
- 1 teaspoon crushed oregano leaves, *or* to taste
- One 8-ounce package of mozzarella
- 1 cup small broccoli florets, steamed tender
- 1 carrot, cut into round slices and cooked
- 4 pitted black olives
- 4 cherry tomatoes
- 1 bunch chives

Delicious!

Geronimo Stilton's Advice

Do you want to know how to be a *gentlemouse*? Here's some cheesy good advice from Yours Truly. When you go to a friend's house for dinner, always remember to pitch in. Ask if you can help set the table, wash the dishes, or take out the garbage. As my great-grandma Tanglefur used to say, "Many paws make LIGHT WORK."

"Hoot if You Like Owls" Pizza

1. Divide the dough into 4 even pieces. On a lightly floured surface, knead and roll each piece into a ball. Cover the balls with a clean, damp dishtowel. Set in a warm place for 20 minutes for the dough to rise. Heat the oven to 450° F.

2. To make each owl pizza: On a floured surface, roll and stretch 1 ball of dough into a 6- to 8-inch circle. Place on an oiled baking sheet. Spread ¼ cup tomato sauce, or more, over the dough, leaving a ½-inch rim around the edge. Drizzle the pizza with a little olive oil, and sprinkle with ¼ teaspoon oregano. Bake the pizza for 10 minutes until the crust is crisp and golden. Carefully remove the pizza from the oven. Let pizza cool for 5 minutes until safe to handle. Place remaining ingredients on the pizza (see photo).

3. Use 1 cup of cooked broccoli florets to make the hair: Arrange the florets around the top half of the outer edge of the pizza.

4. Use soft white cheese to make the owl's feathers: Spread the cheese on the lower half of the pizza.

5. Use 2 slices of hard-boiled egg, 1 pitted green olive, and a hot dog slice to make the eyes: Place the egg slices together under the broccoli. Set a green olive, cut in half, to make the center of the eyes. Cut the hot dog slice in half and place above olives, or use tiny red pepper pieces.

6. Use the red frying pepper to make a beak and mouth: Cut off the pointy end to make the beak and place it between the egg-slice eyes so the beak touches the cheese feathers. Cut a crosswise slice from the pepper (it will look like a ring) and place under the beak. Place tiny pepper strips on either side. Serve immediately.

7. Repeat to make 3 more pizzas. Turn off the oven, and serve the pizzas while warm.

Tasty, and good for you!

Ingredients

Makes 4 individual pizzas

Prep and cook time: 1 hour

- Pizza Dough, see recipe page 68, *or* one 1-pound package of refrigerated ready-made pizza dough
- Flour, for work surface
- Oil, for baking sheet
- 1 cup prepared tomato sauce, *or* more to taste
- Extra-virgin olive oil
- 1 teaspoon oregano leaves
- One 8-ounce package of mozzarella
- 4 cups broccoli florets, steamed tender
- 1 cup crumbled soft white cheese, such as feta or drained ricotta
- 1 large hard-boiled egg, cut in slices
- 4 pitted green olives
- 1 cooked hot dog, sliced into circles
- 4 small red Italian frying peppers

Geronimo Stilton's Advice

My cousin Trap loves to eat. He eats anything and everything. One time, he ate 4 giant cartons of pineapple **cottage cheese** for lunch. Too bad the cottage cheese had gone sour. My cousin spent the next day in bed with a horrible *stomachache*. Don't let the same thing happen to you! Always check the **expiration date**!

Benjamin's Itty-bitty Pizza Stars

1. Heat the oven to 425° F. Break open the biscuit package. Pull each flaky biscuit in half crosswise to make 10 circles. On a lightly floured surface, press each circle evenly until each one is about 3½ inches across.

2. Place circles on a large baking sheet. Cover each pizza with a little tomato sauce. Drizzle with a little olive oil, and sprinkle with a little oregano. Bake the pizzas until they are crisp and golden, about 10 minutes. Remove them from the oven carefully.

3. While the pizzas are baking, cut the American cheese slices using star-shaped cookie cutters (or any other shape that you like). Place the cheese cutouts on top of the hot pizzas. They will melt slightly. Turn off the oven, and serve the pizzas immediately.

These are fabumouse!

Ingredients
Makes 10 tiny pizzas
Prep and cook time: 20 minutes

- One 10.2-ounce package refrigerated big biscuits, 5 per pack
- Flour, for work surface
- ¾ cup prepared tomato sauce, *or more to taste*
- Extra-virgin olive oil
- ¾ teaspoon crushed oregano leaves, *or to taste*
- 4 to 6 slices of American cheese, from an 8-ounce package

Geronimo Stilton's Advice

I love little pizzas. They look so cute and *yummy*. But just because they're little doesn't mean you should scarf them down like the way my uncle Cheesebelly chows at an ALL-YOU-CAN-EAT cheddar buffet. Always remember to take small bites. Food that is swallowed in smaller pieces is easier to digest. Your STOMACH will thank you. And you should never chew with your mouth open. Your friends will thank you for that!

PIZZA TO GO

Two rats walk into a pizza place.

"I'll have 4 large cheese pizzas to go," says the first rat.

"To go?" says the second rat. "I thought we were eating here."

"We are," says the first rat.

"Then why did you order the pizza to go?" says the second.

"Because it is to go. It's to go right into my tummy!" explains the first.

SHOW ME THE DOUGH

Why did the mouse give up his job at the Cheddar Factory to work at the pizzeria?

He wanted to make a lot of dough.

FUR-CHEESE PIZZA

A mouse orders a 4-cheese pizza at the Slice Rat.

When the pizza arrives, the mouse turns green.

Tufts of fur stick out all over the pie.

"I said 4-cheese, not fur-cheese," he moans.

SIMPLE SQUASH

Why did Simplesnout throw the tomato into the air?

He wanted to turn it into squash.

Delicious Soups and Pastas

With a good recipe, you can turn pasta, soup, and vegetables into smiley faces or lakes full of fish. Not only do they look nice, but they're delicious, too! Here are some ideas for whisker-licking good soups and pastas that you can make at home.

Saucy Le Paws's Dreamy Cream Soup

1. Pour canned vegetable broth into a 2-cup measuring cup. Add water to make 2 cups exactly. Pour into a 1½- to 2-quart saucepan. Place the beans in a sieve and drain off all of the liquid. Rinse the beans under cold running water. Add the rinsed beans to the vegetable broth. Cook, covered, over medium-low heat for 5 minutes. Remove from heat and cool slightly.

2. Pour the broth-bean mixture into a blender. Work in two or three batches to prevent the hot liquid from spilling over. Blend until smooth. Return the soup to the saucepan to reheat. Season with salt, to taste.

3. Prepare garnish to make the face: Cut the cherry tomatoes in half to make the cheeks. Cut 1 red pepper slice in the shape of lips. Cut a carrot slice for a nose. Use peas for the eyes and cut little zucchini slivers for the eyebrows. Pour the soup into 2 bowls. Garnish each with prepared vegetables and use drops of pesto sauce to create the hair (see photo). Serve.

Ingredients

Makes 2 servings, 1½ to 2 cups each

Prep and cook time: 20 minutes

- One 13.5-ounce can vegetable broth
- One 15.75-ounce can cannelloni beans
- Salt, to taste
- Peas, carrots, zucchini, and red pepper, steamed tender
- 2 cherry tomatoes
- One 6-ounce jar prepared pesto sauce

It's soup-er good!

Geronimo Stilton's Advice

Do you like to try new foods? I do. As my uncle Nibbles always says, "**Variety** is the spice of life!" So don't just eat that same old cheese sandwich for lunch every day. Try something different. How about using pita bread instead of whole wheat? Or slicing up a mango instead of an apple? Eating can be much more fun when you try NiBBLiNG on different foods once in a while.

Thea's Carrot Soup on the High Seas

1. Clean and peel the carrots. Cut 2 long, thin strips from 1 carrot for the sails of the boats. Set aside. Clean the leek in cold running water.

2. Cut the remaining carrots and the leek into slices. Place in a 2-quart saucepan. Add milk, water, olive oil, and a pinch of salt to the vegetables. Cook, covered, over medium heat for 20 minutes until the vegetables are tender.

3. While the veggies are cooking, make the boats. Cut the zucchini in half lengthwise and scoop out the insides of both halves. Cut one end of each zucchini half into a sharp point to make the prow (front) of the boats (see photo). Push toothpicks through the carrot sails and stick them into each zucchini boat. If you wish, make a flag from your favorite color of construction paper. Stick it on top of the toothpick.

4. Let the pan of cooked vegetables cool. Pour the mixture into a blender. Work in 2 or 3 batches to prevent the liquid from spilling. Blend until creamy. Return blended soup to the pan to reheat. Pour the soup into 2 bowls. Garnish each bowl with a zucchini boat. Add goldfish-shaped crackers to the soup. Serve.

Ingredients

Makes 2 servings, about 1½ to 2 cups each

Prep and cook time: 20 minutes

- 3 to 4 medium-size carrots, about ½ pound
- 1 medium-size leek, halved lengthwise
- 1 cup milk
- 1 cup water
- 1 to 2 tablespoons extra-virgin olive oil, to taste
- Salt, to taste
- 1 small zucchini
- 2 wooden toothpicks
- Construction paper
- Goldfish-shaped crackers

Delicious and nutritious!

Geronimo Stilton's Advice

This recipe isn't good . . . it's **fabumouse**! That's because it not only tastes great but it's good for you, too! It contains VEGETABLES and MILK. Every mouse knows that vegetables are filled with important vitamins. And milk contains calcium, which helps build **strong** mouse bones. Yep, as my aunt Ratsy used to say, "Cats aren't the only ones who need their milk."

Geronimo's Delicious, Good-for-You Pasta

1. Using a 5- or 6-quart saucepan, bring 4 quarts of water to a boil over medium-high heat. Cover the pan so water boils quickly. Add salt to the boiling water, then pasta. Cook, uncovered, stirring frequently to keep the pasta from sticking to the sides of the pan. It will take 10 to 14 minutes to cook.

2. While the pasta is cooking, place the basil leaves in the blender. Add almonds, Parmesan cheese, garlic, olive oil, and salt. Blend until mixture becomes creamy, adding up to 1 tablespoon more of olive oil if needed.

3. Using a small heart-shaped food cutter, or any shape of food cutter you have or like, cut out hearts from the prepared tomato and zucchini. Set aside.

4. When the pasta is tender but still firm to the bite, drain it into a colander. Shake it over the sink to remove water. Place cooked pasta back in the pan and toss it with sauce from the blender. Spoon the hot pasta into 2 serving bowls and top each serving with tomato and zucchini cutouts (see photo).

It's whisker-licking good!

Ingredients

Makes 2 servings

Prep and cook time: 25 minutes

- 4 quarts water
- 2 teaspoons salt
- 2 cups medium-size, assorted-shaped pasta
- 10 fresh basil leaves, washed and dried
- 10 whole, blanched almonds
- 2 tablespoons grated Parmesan cheese
- 1 clove garlic, peeled and crushed
- 2 tablespoons extra-virgin olive oil, plus more if needed
- Pinch of salt
- 2 plum tomatoes, halved, seeds removed, and pressed flat
- Thick strips of skin cut from 1 large zucchini

Geronimo Stilton's Advice

HOLEY CHEESE, I love pasta! Especially when it's mixed with lots and lots of cheese. I love melted cheddar on elbow macaroni, Parmesan cheese on spaghetti, and mozzarella on lasagna. Do you know Tina Spicytail? She's my grandfather William's housekeeper and cook. Tina makes the best lasagna on all of Mouse Island. YUM, YUM!

Benjamin's Fluttery Pasta Butterflies

1. Using a 5- or 6-quart saucepan, bring 4 quarts of water to a boil over medium-high heat. Cover the pan so the water boils quickly.

2. Chop basil, thyme leaves, and marjoram. Place herbs in a large serving bowl and stir in the olive oil. Cut the tomatoes into wedges, each about ½ inch wide. Add tomato wedges to the serving bowl and toss with herb mixture to coat well.

3. Add salt to the boiling water, then pasta. Cook, uncovered, stirring frequently to keep the pasta from sticking to the sides of the pan. It will take 10 to 14 minutes to cook. While the pasta is cooking, place cheese in medium-size bowl and crumble with a fork.

4. When the pasta is tender, but still firm to the bite, drain into a colander. Shake over the sink to remove water. Add the cooked pasta to a serving bowl and toss well with tomatoes. Place the cheese on top. Garnish with a few extra basil leaves (see photo). Toss again before serving.

Holey cheese, this is good!

Ingredients

Makes 6 servings

Prep and cook time: 20 minutes

- 4 quarts water
- 10 fresh basil leaves, well washed, plus more for garnish
- 2 sprigs fresh thyme, or ¾ teaspoon dried thyme
- A few leaves fresh marjoram or ½ teaspoon dried, optional
- 3 tablespoons extra-virgin olive oil
- 3 to 4 medium-size tomatoes, washed, about ¾ pound
- 2 teaspoons salt, plus additional for seasoning
- One 1-pound package bow-tie-shaped pasta, about 4 cups
- ¾-pound soft, dry white cheese, such as feta or ricotta salata, shredded or crumbled

Geronimo Stilton's Advice

Did you ever make up names for your food? When my dear nephew Benjamin was younger, he called broccoli "little trees" and mashed potatoes and gravy "swimming pools." Have fun inventing **funny names** for your favorite dishes. It makes eating a meal something to really squeak about!

29

Tina Spicytail's Famouse Pasta

1. Using a 5- or 6-quart saucepan, bring 4 quarts of water to a boil over medium-high heat. Cover the pan so the water boils quickly. Add salt to the boiling water, then pasta. Cook, uncovered, stirring frequently to keep the pasta from sticking to the sides of the pan. It will take 10 to 14 minutes to cook.

2. While the pasta is cooking, melt butter over medium heat in a 10-inch skillet. Add rosemary, cook for 30 seconds. Add the chicken and the hot dog and cook for 10 minutes, or more, until the chicken is golden and cooked through. Stir frequently while cooking. Once the chicken and hot dog are cooked, place them in a large serving bowl together with any butter left in the skillet.

3. Chop the parsley and sage together, even the powdered sage if you are using it. It will give more flavor to the dish. When the pasta is tender, but still firm to the bite, drain it into a colander. Shake over the sink to remove water. Toss the cooked pasta with the chicken in the serving bowl, adding chopped parsley and sage. Spoon pasta into 4 bowls or plates. Sprinkle each with Parmesan or provolone cheese.

Yum, yum!

Ingredients

Makes 4 servings

Prep and cook time: 20 minutes

- 4 quarts water
- 2 teaspoons salt
- 2 cups pasta (use whatever shape you like best)
- 2 to 3 tablespoons butter
- ½ teaspoon chopped fresh rosemary leaves, or ¼ teaspoon dried
- 1 skinless, boneless chicken breast, about 3 to 4 ounces, cut into bite-size pieces
- 1 hot dog, cut into slices
- ½ cup fresh parsley sprigs
- 3 fresh sage leaves, or ½ teaspoon dried, powdered sage
- ½ cup grated Parmesan or provolone cheese

Geronimo Stilton's Advice

Have you ever tried provolone cheese? It's **WHISKER-LICKING GOOD**. You can sprinkle it over pasta or melt it over your vegetables. The first time I tried provolone I was just a young mouselet. I traded lunch at school with **MY BEST FRIEND**, Scurry. Every day, Scurry's mother packed him a provolone and bologna sandwich, two asparagus spears, and a cookie for lunch. I must admit, I wasn't crazy about the asparagus, but the provolone sandwich was **SUPER-YUMMY**!

Just Joking Around with Geronimo Stilton

SOUP ON THE FLY
A hungry mouse orders a bowl of soup at the Squeak & Chew.
"Holey cheese!" he shrieks when the soup arrives. "There's a fly in my soup! Waiter, change this immediately!"
The waiter scampers toward the kitchen.
"Chef!" he squeaks at the top of his lungs. "A different fly for the customer!"

NOODLES ON THE BRAIN
How did the young rodent learn to eat his macaroni and cheese with a fork?
By using his noodle!

LET THEM EAT MEAT!
Why do gerbils like to get together at the Ratburger?
It's a perfect *meating* place!

SLURP'S UP
Two mice go out to dinner at a fancy restaurant. The first mouse orders a bowl of cheddar soup.
When the soup arrives, he begins to slurp it up noisily.
"Do you have to slurp like that?" the second mouse grumbles.
"No," says the first mouse, jumping on top of the table and doing a headstand. "I can also slurp like this!"

Main Dishes

Meals can be fun with main dishes like these! You can transform eggs into beautiful flowers, vegetables into a buried treasure, and tomatoes into ladybugs. Not only do they look and taste great, but they're good for you, too!

Trap's Buried Treasure

1. Place steamer rack in 1½-quart saucepan. Add just enough water to the pan to touch the bottom of the steamer rack. Cut round slices from the carrot and golden beets; cut small circles from the mozzarella. These will be your "coins." Cut the potato into small diced pieces. Cut the red beet into wedge shapes. Use a tiny melon ball scoop to cut the zucchini into balls or else cut it into slices. The potato, red beet, and zucchini will be your "jewels." You will need approximately 1½ cups of "coins" and "jewels," combined, to fill your treasure chest.

2. Place the carrot circles, golden beet circles, and diced potato on one side of the steamer rack. Place the red beet on the other side of the rack. (Don't let the red beet touch the other vegetables, or they will turn red, too!) Cover the saucepan, and bring the water to a gentle simmer. Cook vegetables for 15 to 20 minutes or until they are tender. Add the zucchini and spinach leaves at the last 2 minutes of cooking time (once again, do not let these touch the red beets). Sprinkle vegetables with a little salt. When the vegetables are cooked, set the pan aside and keep it warm.

3. Preheat a toaster oven or regular oven to 400° F. Cut a 5-inch section from the Italian bread. This will be your "treasure chest." Use a very sharp knife to cut off the loaf ends. Cut the bread in half crosswise (see photo). The domed section will be the "lid." Using a spoon, make a chest by scooping out the soft bread from the bottom section of the bread.

4. Brush all surfaces of the bread very lightly with olive oil. Toast the bread until it is golden brown. Place the treasure chest on a serving plate. Fill the chest with the warm vegetable "coins" and "jewels" and a few mini pretzels. Place the "lid" on top and serve.

Ingredients

Makes 1 serving

Prep and cook time: 30 minutes

- 1 peeled carrot
- 2 small golden beets (if available)
- 3 slices mozzarella, from 8-ounce package
- 1 medium-size potato
- 1 small red beet
- 1 medium-size zucchini
- A few spinach leaves, washed clean
- Pinch of salt
- 1 loaf of Italian bread (at least 5 inches long)
- Extra-virgin olive oil
- A few mini-pretzels (any shape you like)

Scrumptious!

Geronimo Stilton's Advice

When I throw a dinner party, I like to make *place cards* for each of my guests. Sometimes I decorate the cards with pictures. Sometimes I use sparkly glitter glue. Sometimes I cut the cards into funny shapes. One time, I threw a birthday party for my cousin Trap. I cut each card into the shape of a clown. That's because my cousin loves to CLOWN AROUND and play jokes. Too bad most of the jokes are on me!

Benjamin's Wishing Well

1. Cook the rice and peas as directed and keep them warm. Hollow out each zucchini piece. Set aside 2 empty tuna fish cans; make sure that the tuna cans are very clean. Cut out the bottom of each can to make a ring. Set the rings in the center of each serving plate.

2. With a very sharp knife, cut a long strip of ham from 1 slice and set it aside. Cut the remaining ham into ½-inch cubes (see photo #1). Build the wishing wells using ham cubes, placing 3 cubes high all the way around the inside of the molds (see photo #2).

3. In a bowl, toss cooked rice with a little butter, and spoon the rice into the center of ham-lined molds to fill. Carefully lift off the molds. You may have to replace a few bricks. Top each wishing well with more ham cubes and 1 breadstick (see large photo).

4. Fill each zucchini piece with rice and tuck in a tiny strip of ham to make a handle. Surround each serving with cooked peas tossed in a little butter.

Note: If you can't find a tuna can from which you can cut off both top and bottom, pack rice into a clean tuna can and unmold it onto a serving plate. Place ham cubes around the rice to make a wishing well.

Ingredients

Makes 2 servings

Prep and cook time: 30 minutes

- ⅔ cup long-grain rice, cooked according to directions
- One 10-ounce package frozen peas, cooked according to directions
- 2 pieces zucchini, each 1½ inches in length
- 2 slices cooked ham, about ⅓-inch thick, each weighing 3 ounces
- Butter, to taste, optional
- Two 6-ounce empty tuna cans (see note)
- 2 breadsticks

1

2

Enjoy!

Geronimo Stilton's Advice

For a picky eater, try making this **SPECIAL DISH.** Fill a stalk of celery with some peanut butter. Then stick **raisins** onto the peanut butter. Do you know what I call this dish? Ants on a log! Even a 'fraidy mouse like me loves this creepy-crawly treat!

Thea's Flower Blossom

1. Make flower petals using a 2½-inch cookie cutter or the rim of a drinking glass to cut 2 circles from each bread slice. You will have 8 circles. Place the bread circles on a baking sheet from the toaster oven and toast them until they are golden. You may have to do this in 2 batches.

2. In a small skillet, heat butter over medium heat. Crack the egg into the skillet and cook sunny-side up until egg white is firm and yolk begins to set.

3. Using a wide metal spatula, remove the egg from the skillet and place it in the center of a serving plate. Surround the egg yolk with toast circles to make petals, as pictured. Add chives for garnish, green beans for the stem, and basil leaves for the leaves (see photo).

Ingredients

Makes 1 serving

Prep and cook time: 20 minutes

- 4 large slices soft white bread, or 8 medium slices
- 2 tablespoons butter or olive oil
- 1 large egg
- 2 chives, for garnish
- 2 cooked green beans
- 2 basil leaves

An egg-cellent meal!

Geronimo Stilton's Advice

Here's a little trick that I learned from my dear **aunt Sweetfur**. To find out if your eggs are fresh, gently place them in a bowl filled with water. If the eggs sink to the bottom, it means they are still fresh. If they FLOAT TO THE TOP, it's better to throw them out. Eggs should have the expiration date printed clearly on the carton.

Nibblette's Scurrying Ladybugs

Nibblette makes this dish into a healthy, tasty lunch by adding a simple tossed green salad and crusty whole wheat bread.

1. Cut the tomatoes in half widthwise (see photo). Scoop them out and discard the seeds. Place the tomatoes cut-side down on a paper towel to drain.

2. In a small bowl, combine the mozzarella, basil, and mayonnaise so the mixture holds together. Spoon the mixture into the hollowed-out tomato halves, dividing evenly. Place 2 tomato halves, cut-side down, on each of 2 serving plates.

3. Cut 2 black olives in half widthwise. Place the olive halves at the tops of each tomato half to form the head of the ladybug. Cut the remaining olives into tiny cubes.

4. Decorate the ladybugs by using a toothpick. Dip it first in mayonnaise and then dab onto the back of the ladybug to make a dot. Place 1 olive cube on top of each dot. Place 2 dots of mayonnaise on each black olive half to make eyes. Set tiny basil leaves on either side of each tomato ladybug to make three-leaf clovers.

Ingredients

Makes 2 servings

Prep and cook time: 20 minutes

- 2 ripe plum tomatoes
- ½ cup finely diced mozzarella
- 2 tablespoons chopped basil leaves
- 2 tablespoons mayonnaise, plus more for decoration
- 3 to 4 pitted black olives
- Tiny whole basil leaves

Get them while they last!

Geronimo Stilton's Advice

Every mouse knows it's **important** to have good table manners. Well, every mouse except my cousin Trap, that is. The other night, he was invited to a very *fancy wedding* and was almost kicked out of the reception! First he wiped his paws on the silk tablecloth, then he **burped** after sipping his mozzarella shake, then he stood on the table to tell a joke. How embarrassing! Can you believe we are related?

Pinky Pick's Goofy Octopuses

1. Place potatoes in a large pot and cover with cold water. Add a little salt to the water. Bring pot to a boil and cook for about 30 minutes, until the potatoes are soft. Drain the potatoes, and then, while hot, mash smooth. Add a little salt, pepper, and butter. In a separate covered pan, cook the spinach in ½ cup of boiling water, about 2 minutes. Drain off any extra liquid. Add a little salt, pepper, and oil. Keep warm when finished cooking.

2. Cut 4 hot dogs in half lengthwise. Stop a finger-width from the end. Slice each hot dog 3 more times lengthwise to make 8 tentacles (see photo #1). Cut the remaining 4 hot dogs in half crosswise. Cut the tentacles the same way as with the first 4 hot dogs.

3. Using a potato peeler, cut thin strips lengthwise from carrots. Cut the carrot strips into 12 fish shapes (see photo #2). Set aside.

4. In a skillet, using a little olive oil over medium heat, cook hot dogs by squashing them down from the top so tentacles stick out to the sides. The hot dogs are done when they are warmed through and just start to brown. Serve 1 large and 2 small hot dog octopuses on a sea of mashed potatoes. Place spinach in 3 piles to make seaweed. Add 3 carrot fish. Using toothpick, add mustard dots to make octopus eyes (see large photo).

Ingredients

Makes 4 servings

Prep and cook time: 40 minutes

- 2 pounds (about 6 medium) all-purpose potatoes, cut into quarters, peeled and cooked
- Salt, pepper, butter and extra-virgin olive oil, to taste
- 1 pound fresh spinach, washed
- 8 large hot dogs
- 2 carrots, peeled
- Mild yellow mustard

1

2

Fun!

Geronimo Stilton's Advice

Don't pull out your fur if a recipe doesn't come out **exactly** the way you planned. Everyone makes mistakes. Sometimes the only way to learn is by *TRIAL AND ERROR*. As my cousin Plumpypaws would say, "If at first you don't succeed, try eating three bowls of macaroni and cheese!"

Grandfather William's "Big Cheese" Clock Pie

1. Heat the oven to 400° F. Roll out ⅔ of the pie dough recipe on a lightly floured surface. Use the dough to line a 9-inch pie plate. Save the trimmings and extra dough to make the clock hands and numbers. Prick the bottom of the crust with a fork. Freeze the crust for 15 minutes, then bake it for 15 minutes, remove it from the oven, and let it cool.

2. Wash the spinach thoroughly and pat dry. Chop the leaves into small pieces. Cook in ½ cup boiling water in a covered pan until tender, about 2 minutes. Drain off any extra liquid, and place the spinach in a large bowl. Beat in ricotta and Parmesan cheeses, and 2 eggs.

3. Sprinkle ham over the bottom of the crust. Top with spinach-cheese mixture. Roll out the remaining dough and cut it into clock hands and numbers. Brush with beaten egg yolk. Place the hands and numbers on the pie (see photo). Bake for 20 minutes or until crust is golden brown and filling is set.

Note: There are usually 2 ready-made piecrusts per package. Use one to line the pie plate and the other to make the clock hands and numbers. If there are more piecrusts in the package, put the leftover ones back in the freezer to use at a later date. Make sure to return them to the freezer before they thaw!

Eat up!

Ingredients

Makes 4 servings

Prep and cook time: 45 to 50 minutes

- Tender Piecrust Dough, see page 69, *or* one 15.5-ounce package ready-made piecrust
- Flour, for work surface
- 8 ounces fresh spinach
- One 8-ounce container ricotta cheese
- ½ cup grated Parmesan cheese
- 2 large eggs, plus one extra egg yolk
- ¾ cup finely diced cooked ham, about 3 ounces

Geronimo Stilton's Advice

One thing you should know about me: I am a *gentlemouse*. When I go out to eat, I never gulp down my food like a starving rat. I take small, polite bites. And I always remember to say **PLEASE**, **you're welcome**, and **THANK YOU**.

Just Joking Around with Geronimo Stilton

THREE BLIND COOKS

A mouse goes out to eat at the House of Cheese. When the waiter brings his meal, the food looks awful. The bread is burned. The eggs are uncooked. And the spinach pie has a whisker sticking out of it.

"This is a disgrace!" the mouse shrieks. "What happened to this place? It used to be a four-star ratstaurant!"

The waiter shakes his head and sighs. "I told the boss not to hire those Three Blind Mice," he mutters.

KICK UP YOUR CHEESE!

Where do mozzarella sticks like to dance?
At a cheese ball.

NO-BRAINER

Three mice are lost in the hot Mousehara Desert.

"I wish I had a frosty mozzarella shake," moans Whiskers.

"I wish I had a cheddar Popsicle," wails Nibbles.

"I wish I had a car door," says Cheesebrain, sighing.

The first two mice stare at Cheesebrain.

"A car door? What would you do with a car door?" asks Whiskers.

"Roll down the window, of course! I'm roasting!" squeaks Cheesebrain.

Delicious Desserts

There's no better way to end a meal than with a sweet, tasty dessert! Here are some you can make at home. They're sure to impress your family and friends — rodent's word of honor!

Aunt Sweetfur's Pudding Bears

1. To prepare vanilla bears: Pour contents of the vanilla pudding mix into a small saucepan. Add 2 cups of cold milk and stir until the powder is dissolved. Cook over medium heat, stirring constantly, until the pudding mixture comes to a full boil.

2. Turn heat to low and continue stirring the pudding to cook at a gentle boil for 3 to 4 minutes. Pour the pudding mixture into two 1-cup bear molds. Be careful — the pudding is very hot.

3. Prepare the chocolate bears the same way as the vanilla bears. Pour the cooked chocolate pudding into 2 more 1-cup bear molds.

4. As soon as the bears have cooled a little, chill them in the refrigerator until they set firm and are really cold. This will take at least an hour. When ready to eat, unmold each bear onto serving plates and decorate with candy-coated chocolates (see photo).

Ingredients

Makes 4 servings

Prep time: 15 minutes plus 1 hour to cool

- One 3-ounce package vanilla pudding mix
- 4 cups milk
- One 3-ounce package chocolate pudding mix
- Candy-coated chocolate, for decoration

Beary, beary good!

Geronimo Stilton's Advice

When you're cooking, the kitchen is no place to kick up your paws. Once, my cousin Twinklepaws was practicing *ballet* in her kitchen. She accidentally kicked over a pot that was cooking on the stove. It was filled with boiling water! Luckily, Twinklepaws was OK. But she could have been seriously **BURNED**. Always remember to keep pot handles turned inward. And never pick up a hot pot without putting your paws in a pair of oven mitts.

Geronimo's Smiley-Face Crepes

1. Prepare crepe batter in a medium bowl by stirring together flour, eggs, and milk. Beat the mixture until it is smooth and as thick as heavy cream. Beat in melted butter.

2. Heat a nonstick 8-inch skillet. Add a little butter to the pan and swirl to coat. Then add about 3 tablespoons of batter and swirl it in the pan to make a thin crepe. Cook the crepe until bubbles appear, then flip it and cook the other side until golden brown. Repeat to make 8 crepes total. If the batter thickens while standing, thin by adding a little more milk.

3. Place a crepe on each of 4 plates. Spread some jam on each. Cut eyes and mouth from each of other 4 crepes (see photo). Be sure to be extra careful with the knife.

4. Place a cutout crepe on top of a jam-covered crepe. Place ¼ cup of coconut and 1 tablespoon of almonds on each crepe to make hair. Add tiny berries for the eyes and a raspberry for the nose. Sprinkle with confectioners' sugar and serve.

Ingredients

Makes 4 servings

Prep and cook time: 30 minutes

- ½ cup all-purpose flour
- 2 large eggs, beaten
- ¾ cup milk, plus more if needed
- 2 tablespoons butter, melted, plus more for cooking
- ½ cup raspberry jam, or more to taste
- 1 cup shaved or grated coconut
- ¼ cup sliced toasted almonds (unsalted)
- 8 tiny berries, such as red currants or blueberries
- 4 raspberries
- Confectioners' sugar

Smile—it's time to eat!

Geronimo Stilton's Advice

As I always say to my favorite nephew, Benjamin, **breakfast** is very important for providing the **energy** you will need to face the day. Plus, it's delicious! Once in a while, try to **prepare** breakfast for your family. It's a thoughtful gesture that everyone will appreciate.

Mousella's Mini Mushroom Houses

1. Place the ice cream in the refrigerator to soften slightly. Chop pistachio nuts and divide them between 4 dessert plates to make a "lawn." Place a few red berries on one side of each plate. Set the plates in the refrigerator to chill.

2. Drain 4 peach halves and 4 apricot halves from their cans and pat them dry with paper towels. Using a toothpick dipped in the vanilla frosting, place dots on top of halves (see photo).

3. Working quickly, place a large ½-cup scoop and a small ¼-cup scoop of ice cream on each plate. Top with a peach and an apricot half.

Ingredients

Makes 4 servings

Prep time: 10 minutes

- 1 quart vanilla ice cream
- 1 cup green pistachio nuts without shells
- A few red currant berries or raspberries
- 4 peach halves, from 15.25-ounce can
- 4 apricot halves, from 15.25-ounce can
- One 16-ounce can of ready-to-spread vanilla frosting

Sweet and tasty!

Geronimo Stilton's Advice

I'd like to give you a suggestion: When you do something, try to do it with *love*! First of all, it will come out better, and second, everyone will appreciate what you did even more. For example, the other day my friend Benny Bluewhiskers offered me several beautiful pieces of fresh CHEESE on a dish decorated with LEAVES and flowers. It looked like a green field that I would have happily rolled in. Sometimes a small act of kindness can make someone's day more enjoyable!

Benjamin's Cheesecake Butterflies

1. Peel and core 2 pears. Cut the pears into cubes and add them to the food processor along with the peach halves and 2 tablespoons of brown sugar. Process at high speed until smooth.

2. In a medium-size bowl, beat together the ricotta cheese, cream cheese, and remaining ¼ cup of brown sugar until smooth. Stir in the fruit mixture. Divide between four 1-cup dessert dishes. Smooth the tops. Chill the fruit-cheese mixture in the refrigerator while preparing the rest of the fruit.

3. Cut the papaya into 8 slices. Remove the stems from the strawberries. Peel and slice the kiwifruits into 8 slices. Peel the remaining pear and cut it lengthwise into 16 thin strips.

4. Arrange the cut fruit on top of each dessert dish to make a butterfly (see photo). Eat immediately or chill until after dinner. Sprinkle with multicolored sugar sprinkles just before serving.

Sweet!

Ingredients

Makes 4 servings

Prep time: 45 minutes

- 3 medium-size firm but ripe pears, about ¾ pound
- 4 peach halves, from 15.25-ounce can
- 2 tablespoons brown sugar, plus ¼ cup brown sugar, firmly packed
- 1½ cups ricotta cheese
- One 6-ounce package cream cheese, softened
- 1 small papaya, peeled
- 8 small strawberries
- 2 kiwifruits
- Multicolored sugar sprinkles

Geronimo Stilton's Advice

Learn to listen to your tummy. My tummy GROWLS and GRUMBLES when I'm hungry. Sometimes it sounds just like an angry bear. And I don't mean a cute, cuddly, stuffed one! Try to nibble on small healthy snacks throughout the day. Your tummy will thank you for it by staying as quiet as a mouse.

Pinky Pick's Delicious Cheesecake Doll Faces

1. Peel and core 2 pears. Cut the pears into cubes and add them to a food processor along with the peach halves and 2 tablespoons of brown sugar. Process at high speed until smooth.

2. In a medium-size bowl, beat together the ricotta cheese, cream cheese, and remaining ¼ cup of brown sugar until smooth. Stir in the fruit mixture. Divide between four 1-cup dessert dishes. Smooth the tops. Chill the fruit-cheese mixture in the refrigerator while preparing the rest of the fruit.

3. Working in a bowl, make a little hollow in the almond paste; add 6 drops of red and 3 drops of yellow food coloring. Carefully knead the paste to make an orange color. Add more food coloring if needed. Roll the paste into mini carrot shapes. These are the eyebrows.

4. Use meringue cookies and orange hard candies for the eyes. Set a piece of striped hard candy in place for the nose. Cut an extra pear into slices for a mouth, and add sliced strawberries for the lips. Then add some chocolate sprinkles for the hair (see photo).

Fabumouse!

Ingredients

Makes 4 servings
Prep time: 45 minutes

- 3 medium-size, firm but ripe pears, about ¾ pound
- 4 peach halves, from 15.25-ounce can
- 2 tablespoons brown sugar, plus ¼ cup brown sugar, firmly packed,
- 1½ cups ricotta cheese
- One 6-ounce package cream cheese, softened
- 4 ounces almond paste or marzipan, from 8-ounce package
- Red and yellow food coloring
- 8 tiny store-bought meringue cookies
- 8 orange or lemon hard candies
- 4 striped hard candies
- 2 strawberries, sliced
- Chocolate sprinkles

Geronimo Stilton's Advice

I love sweets. But too many **sweets** can make you feel sick. Plus, who wants to be a roly-poly rodent? Cookies, cake, and candy are good once in a while. But fresh fruits like grapes, **STRAWBERRIES**, bananas, and apples can be just as yummy — and as sweet.

Trap's Colorful Clown Cake

1. Heat the oven to 350° F. Using an 8-cup clown-shaped pan, butter the inside well, getting it into every nook and cranny. Then add flour and shake the pan to coat it evenly. Turn the pan upside down to remove any extra flour.

2. Make the cake batter according to directions for the Simple Sponge Cake. Add the batter to the floured pan. Bake for 35 to 40 minutes until the cake is golden brown and the top springs back when lightly touched. Cool the pan on a wire rack for 5 minutes. Turn the pan upside down to remove the cake. Cool the cake completely on wire rack before decorating.

3. Decorate the cake by carefully following the photo. If you don't have a star decorating tip and piping bag, swirl frosting onto the cake using the tip of a small teaspoon or spatula.

4. First use vanilla frosting to decorate the white sections of the clown face. In a small bowl, color half of the second can of vanilla frosting yellow with food coloring, and use it to make the hair. Color a little of the remaining vanilla frosting pink using red food coloring. Use the pink frosting to make the mouth and nose.

5. Spread chocolate frosting to make a hat, and top with chopped pistachios. Add the multicolored sprinkles to make the collar.

6. Fill a piping bag containing a plain decorating tip with ¾ cup of chocolate frosting. Pipe chocolate lines on the clown face as shown in the photo. Or place the frosting in a plastic sandwich bag. Seal the bag by pressing the frosting into the bottom corner. Snip the corner to make a tiny hole before piping in the lines.

Ingredients

Makes 6 to 8 servings

Prep, cook, and decorating time: 2 hours 20 minutes (Or you can make the cake a day ahead, then you will need only 30 minutes.)

- Butter and flour for coating pan
- Simple Sponge Cake, see page 70
- Star and plain decorating tips and piping bags
- Two 16-ounce cans of ready-to-spread vanilla frosting
- Yellow and red food coloring
- One 16-ounce can of ready-to-spread chocolate frosting
- ⅓ cup finely chopped pistachio nuts
- Multicolored sugar sprinkles

Geronimo Stilton's Advice

If this is your first time cooking, it's always a good idea to start with an **EASY** recipe. Remember, even the best chefs had to start somewhere. My great-aunt Cookiewhisker makes the most *delicious* cheesecake, but she wasn't always a great cook. Once, she tried to bake a batch of cheddar rolls and she burned them to a crisp. Her mouse hole smelled like burned cheese for weeks! PEE-YEW!

Thea's Tasty Merry-go-round

1. Let the cookie dough soften slightly at room temperature. Use ⅔ of the dough to line a 9-inch shallow tart pan or an 8-inch pie pan. Use your fingers to press the dough directly into the pan. Press evenly over the bottom and sides. Place the pan in the freezer for 10 minutes.

2. Heat the oven to 400° F. Bake the chilled tart shell for 15 minutes, or until it is crisp and golden brown. Let it cool in the pan on a wire rack for 5 minutes. Remove the crust from the pan and place it on a serving plate. Place the plate in the refrigerator to cool.

3. On a lightly floured surface, roll the remaining dough to ⅓-inch thickness. Using people- and leaf-shaped cookie cutters, cut out 12 people shapes, and some leaf shapes. Use a wide spatula to place the cookies on large baking sheet. Bake the cookies for 10 to 12 minutes, depending on their size, until they are crisp and golden brown. Using the spatula, place the cookies on a wire rack to cool.

4. Cover the bottom of the chilled tart shell with the chocolate-nut spread or peanut butter. Top evenly with raspberry jam. Set the cooled people- and leaf-shaped cookies in place (see photo). If there is time, chill the tart for a few minutes before serving.

Ingredients

Makes 6 servings

Prep and cook time: 35 minutes

- Lemony Cookie Dough, see page 71, made ahead of time and chilled
- Flour, for work surface
- 1 cup chocolate-nut spread, or peanut butter
- 1½ cups raspberry jam, or more to taste

Tart and tasty!

Geronimo Stilton's Advice

When sitting at the table, try to appreciate what was prepared, and keep in mind how much **WORK** went into every dish. If you really like a dish, ask for a little more, but if it's truly something you **dislike**, try to at least finish what you have on your plate.

Creepella von Cacklefur's Personalized Cookies

1. Heat the oven to 400° F. Cut homemade or store-bought dough into 4 balls. Work with 1 ball of the dough at a time, keeping the remainder chilled.

2. Roll the ball of dough out on a lightly floured surface and cut out 12 cookies using a 2½-inch fluted or plain cookie cutter. Place the cookies on a large baking sheet with a wide spatula. Bake for 10 to 12 minutes until they are golden brown. Using a wide spatula, place the cookies on a wire rack to cool completely. Repeat to make 12 more cookies. Make sure the baking sheet is cool before reusing.

3. Working with the third batch of dough, cut out 12 cookies, but also cut out eyes and a mouth with a tiny leaf-shaped cookie cutter or the tip of a sharp knife. Using a wide spatula, place the cookies on a cooled baking sheet. Bake and cool as above. Repeat with the fourth ball of dough to make 12 more face-shaped cookies. It is important to save the scraps of cookie dough. Chill the dough before rerolling it to make more cookies.

4. Place a little of your favorite cookie filling — chocolate-nut spread, peanut butter, or jam — on the bottom of 24 plain cookies. Top each with a face-shaped cookie and sprinkle with confectioners' sugar before serving.

Ingredients

Makes 24 cookies

Prep and cook time: 40 minutes

- Lemony Cookie Dough, see page 71, or one 18-ounce package refrigerated vanilla cookie dough
- Flour, for work surface
- ¾ cup chocolate-nut spread, peanut butter, or your favorite jam
- Confectioners' sugar, for sprinkling

These cookies will make you smile!

Geronimo Stilton's Advice

Here's something to squeak about. You can change the ingredients in this recipe to make everyone happy. For instance, if you know your dad likes peanut butter, you can add peanut butter instead of the chocolate-nut spread. Or if your mom loves **APRICOT** jam, you can use that flavor. Now that's enough to put a *Smile* on any rodent's snout!

Grandfather William's Favorite Animal Cookies

1. Heat the oven to 400° F. Cut homemade or store-bought dough into 4 balls. Work with 1 ball at a time. Keep the remainder chilled.

2. Roll the ball of dough out on a lightly floured surface. Using animal-shaped cookie cutters, about 2½ inches in size, cut out 12 cookies. Using a wide spatula, place the cookies on large baking sheet. Bake for 10 to 12 minutes until the cookies are golden brown.

3. Using a wide spatula, place the cookies on a wire rack to cool completely. Repeat to make more cookies, working with only 1 ball of the dough at a time. Make sure the baking sheet is cool before reusing. It is important to save the scraps of cookie dough. Chill the excess dough before rerolling to make more cookies.

4. Decorate cooled cookies by placing ¾ cup of chocolate frosting in a plastic bag. Press frosting into the bottom corner of the bag. Snip off the corner to make a tiny hole in the bag, and use it to pipe outlines of animals on each cookie.

Ingredients

Makes 48 or more cookies

Prep and cook time: 40 to 50 minutes

- Lemony Cookie Dough, see page 71, *or* one 18-ounce package refrigerated vanilla cookie dough
- Flour, for work surface
- One 16-ounce can ready-to-spread chocolate frosting

Eat up!

Geronimo Stilton's Advice

Don't be a messy mousey! Always remember to clean up in the kitchen. If you don't, someone may get hurt. Like the time I was visiting my friend Saucy Le Paws. Saucy spilled some **oil** on the floor when he was making a cheese soufflé. Guess who stepped in the oil? That's right, Yours Truly. *I WENT DOWN* like a lightweight rat in a heavyweight boxing match. **Youch!**

Just Joking Around with Geronimo Stilton

ME-SOUR!
What did the mouse call the cat that ate a plate of lemon tarts?
A real sourpuss!

FRUIT ON WHEELS
Why wouldn't the mouse buy a used car from a fresh fruit dealer?
He didn't want to end up with a lemon!

FRIES IN THE SKIES
A hungry rodent pulls up to the drive-through window at the Burger Rat.
  "I'll have 3 cheeseburgers, 2 mozzarella milk shakes, and a side of cheddar
  fries," he orders. "And make it snappy."
The mouse behind the window gets out a slingshot and quickly shoots the food
  into the sky.
"Hey, why did you throw away my order?" squeaks the hungry rodent.
"I thought you wanted fast food," explains the Burger Rat mouse.

Basic Recipes

Pizza Dough

1. Place warm water in 3-quart mixing bowl. Sprinkle with dry yeast and sugar. Using a wooden spoon, stir to mix well. Let the mixture stand for 5 minutes. Mixture will begin to be frothy (see photo #1).

2. Slowly stir the flour and salt into the yeast mixture. Use your hands to knead the dough. You may not need to use all of the flour. The dough should be soft and pliable, yet leave the sides of the bowl.

3. Knead for 5 minutes until the dough leaves your fingers. If it sticks, add a little more flour. Turn the dough onto a lightly floured surface. Knead for 5 minutes more, until the dough is smooth and elastic. Shape into a ball.

4. Clean the mixing bowl. Lightly oil the inside of the bowl. Place the dough into the bowl; cut a cross on the top (see photo #2). Cover the bowl with oiled plastic wrap or a clean, damp dishtowel.

5. Set the bowl of dough in a warm, draft-free place. After 1 hour, the dough will have doubled in volume and, when lightly pressed, your finger will leave a mark in it.

6. Turn the dough onto a floured surface. Knead again until smooth. It is now ready to use in any of the pizza recipes.

! Note: Or you may shape the dough into an 8-inch round and lightly cut the top in a tic-tac-toe design with a sharp knife. Cover with oiled plastic wrap or a clean, damp dishtowel and let rise again until doubled in bulk, about 45 minutes to 1 hour. Heat the oven to 400° F. Bake the dough for 30 to 35 minutes until golden and sounds hollow when tapped (see photo #3).

Ingredients

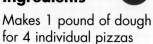

Makes 1 pound of dough for 4 individual pizzas

Prep time: 1½ hours

- 2 cups warm (not hot) water, 95–105° F
- 1 package active dry yeast
- 1 teaspoon sugar
- 4 to 5 cups all-purpose flour, plus extra as needed
- 1 teaspoon salt, optional
- Oil, for bowl

1

2

3

Tender Piecrust Dough

It's messy to make this dough on the table, as the photographs show. So be a squeaky-clean mouse and make it in a bowl!

1. Place the flour, salt (if using), and butter pieces into a 3-quart mixing bowl. Using your fingertips, rub the ingredients together until the mixture resembles crumbly coarse cornmeal (see photo #1).

2. Sprinkle ice-cold water over the flour mixture, stirring in with your fingertips or with a fork to mix well (see photo #2). Using your fingertips and working quickly, lightly knead the dough to form a smooth ball (see photo #3).

3. Wrap the pastry dough in plastic wrap. Refrigerate for 30 minutes or until ready to use.

Makes two 9-inch pie crusts

Prep and chill time: 45 minutes

- 4 cups all-purpose flour
- 1⅓ cups butter, at room temperature and cut into small pieces
- 1 teaspoon salt, optional
- ½ cup ice-cold water

Simple Sponge Cake

It is important to sift the flour before measuring it so you will have a deliciously light cake.

1. Heat the oven to 350° F. Lightly butter an 8-inch by 2-inch round cake pan or 8-inch springform pan. Add 2 tablespoons flour to the pan, shaking to coat the bottom and sides. Turn the pan upside down and shake out any extra flour.

2. In a 3-quart mixing bowl using an electric mixer at high speed, beat together the eggs and sugar. The batter should be light and fluffy, and almost white in color. It will take about 5 minutes (see photo #1).

3. To test if the batter is beaten enough, scoop up a spoonful and drop the mixture back in the bowl. The batter should stay on top (see photo #2). If it sinks, keep beating it. Beat in the vanilla and salt.

4. Using a wooden spoon or wide rubber spatula, gently stir in 1 cup of flour a little bit at a time. Take care that the batter does not lose volume and that it stays fluffy (see photo #3).

5. Spoon the batter into the prepared pan, smoothing it evenly with a spatula. Bake for 25 to 30 minutes until the cake is golden brown and the top springs back when lightly touched.

6. Remove the cake from the pan immediately. Let it cool completely on a wire rack before decorating.

Ingredients

Makes one 8-inch round cake

Prep and cook time: 45 to 50 minutes plus 1 hour to cool cake

- Butter, for greasing pan
- 2 tablespoons all-purpose flour, for cake pan
- 4 large eggs
- 1 cup sugar
- 1 teaspoon vanilla extract *or* 1 teaspoon grated lemon peel
- Pinch salt
- 1 cup sifted all-purpose flour

Lemony Cookie Dough

1. Place the flour and butter in 3-quart mixing bowl. Using your fingertips, rub the flour and butter together until the mixture resembles crumbly coarse cornmeal. Stir in sugar, grated lemon peel, and salt (see photo #1).

2. Make a well, or hole, in the center of the flour mixture. Place egg yolks and vanilla into the well (see photo #2). Using your fingertips, quickly and evenly mix the dough together. Shape the dough into a smooth ball (see photo #3).

3. Wrap the cookie dough in plastic wrap. Refrigerate for 30 minutes or until ready to use.

Ingredients

Makes 1 pie shell and 12 cookies, or 24 sandwich cookies

Prep and chill time: 45 minutes

- 4 cups all-purpose flour
- 1 cup butter, cut into small pieces, at room temperature
- 1 cup sugar
- Grated lemon peel from one large lemon
- Pinch salt
- 4 large egg yolks
- 1½ teaspoons vanilla extract

Thanks for cooking with us!

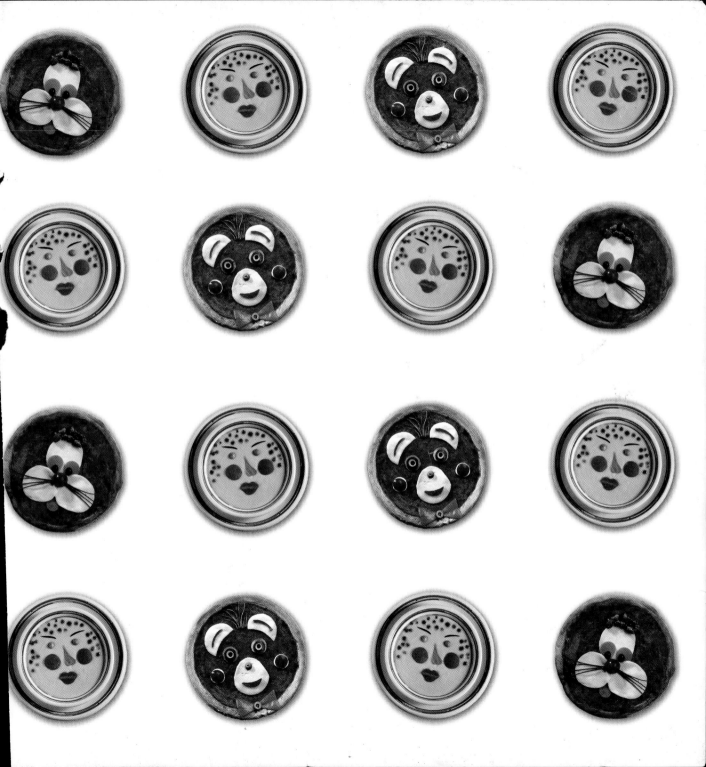